W9-AVC-690

FIRST GRADERS from MARS

Episode 2: The Problem with Pelly

Story by SHANA COREY

Pictures by MARK TEAGUE

SCHOLASTIC PRESS • NEW YORK

Library of Congress Cataloging-in-Publication Data
Corey, Shana.
First graders from Mars episode 2: the problem with Pelly / story by Shana Corey ; pictures by Mark Teague.—1st ed. p. cm.
Summary: Pelly feels miserable because she looks different from her martian classmates, but a glamorous opera singer who visits her class shows Pelly that her differences make her special.
ISBN 0-439-26632-7
[1. Self-acceptance—Fiction. 2. Individuality—Fiction. 3. Schools—Fiction. 4. Mars (Planet)—Fiction.] I. Teague, Mark ill. II. Title PZ7.C8155 Fk 2002 [E]—dc21 2001020842
10 9 8 7 6 5 4 3 2 1 02 03 04 05 06
Printed in Mexico 49
First edition, February 2002
The text type was set in 18-point Martin Gothic Medium.
Book design by Kristina Albertson

To Myra and Erika

— SC

To Imanuel

— MT

Pod 1 was getting ready
for a special visitor.
She was a singer
with the Grand Martian Opera.

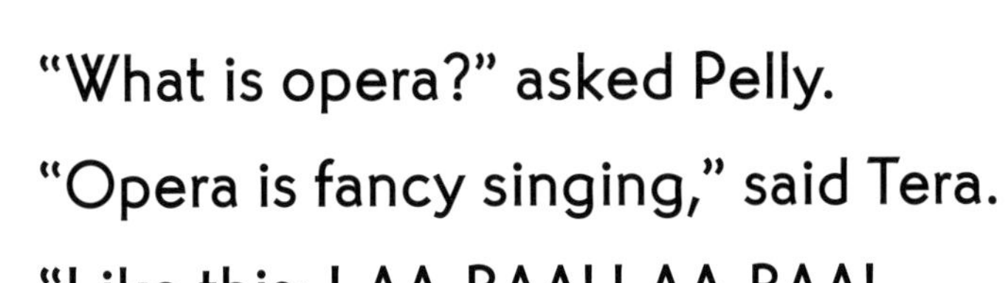

"What is opera?" asked Pelly.

"Opera is fancy singing," said Tera.

"Like this: LAA-BAA! LAA-BAA!

LAA-BAA!" she sang.

Horus covered his ears.

The plants covered theirs, too.

Everyone wanted to
make a good impression.
They cleaned out
their thinking capsules.
They practiced playing
their instruments.
They drew pictures
to hang on the walls.

"What is *that*?" asked Tera
when she saw Pelly's picture.
"That is my family," said Pelly.

Tera held up her own picture.
She and her parents
had matching tentacles.
The baby had two heads.
"This is what normal families
look like," said Tera.
"Your family is weird."

Horus glared at Tera.

"Pelly's family is not weird," he said.

He looked at Pelly's picture.

"They're just different."

Pelly frowned.

She didn't want to be different.

She wanted to be normal.

She looked at her picture again.

Maybe her family *was* weird.

Maybe *she* was weird.

She threw away her picture

so the special visitor wouldn't see it.

After school,
Pelly's mom picked her up.
The fluffernobbin on her head
bobbed up and down in the breeze.

Pelly looked around.
None of the other mothers
had fluffernobbins.
They all had regular tentacles.
"I'll just go in and say 'meep meep'
to Ms. Vortex," said Pelly's mom.
"Nobo!" said Pelly. "I think
she's busy. Let's go!"
She hopped into the flying cup
and shut the hatch.

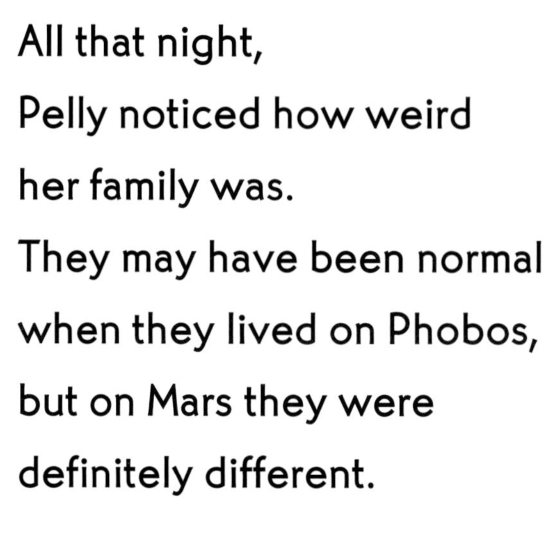

All that night,
Pelly noticed how weird
her family was.
They may have been normal
when they lived on Phobos,
but on Mars they were
definitely different.

Whenever they spoke,
their mouths moved
like normal martians'.
But the words drifted out
of their fluffernobbins.
"Wabatch this!" said Pelly's brother.
He blew a milk bubble
through his fluffernobbin.
Pelly sank down in her seat
and sighed.

Pelly didn't want the special visitor
to think she was weird.
So the next morning,
she put three rubber bands
around her fluffernobbin.
Then she went down to breakfast.

"Your beautiful fluffernobbin!"

said Pelly's mom.

"What was wrong with it

the way it was?"

Pelly looked at her mom sadly.

She had no idea.

After breakfast, Pelly's mom
took her to school.
Pelly looked
at her fluffernobbin
one last time.
It was perfect!
She skipped all the way
into Pod 1.
She felt wonderful.
She felt light as air.
But best of all . . .
she felt normal.

Then she saw Tera.
"What is *that*
on your head?"
asked Tera.
"Tentacles," said Pelly.

Only the rubber bands
muffled the words.
So it came out "Twerp-cicles."
"Nice twerp-cicles," said Tera.

No one else liked
Pelly's tentacles, either.
"You were fine the way
you were," said Horus.
"Juice-bean-ice," said Pelly.
(She meant: "You're just being nice.")

“We can’t understand

what you’re saying,” said Ms. Vortex.

Pelly scribbled on her pad:

I’LL WRITE NOTES.

At lunchtime,
Horus gave Pelly
a slice of his
pepper-and-pancake pie.
The pepper tickled
Pelly's nose.
"A-a-achoo-boo!" she said.
Pop!
The rubber bands
flew off her fluffernobbin.

Ms. Vortex
was *not* amused.

"That's it, Pelly," said Ms. Vortex.
"Nobo more tentacles."
"But I will be the only one
without them!" cried Pelly.
"And the only one with that
fluffer-whatever," Tera pointed out.

After lunch, Ms. Vortex
called Pod 1 together.
"Time to get ready
for our special visitor."
"I have never met
a famous singer," said Horus.
"Me neither," said Pelly. "But then,
famous singers probably
stay away from weirdos."
"I bet she likes me best," said Tera.
"I have a lovely singing voice."

Ms. Vortex passed out instruments.
"We'll play backup," she said.
Everyone started tuning up.
Suddenly, the door opened.
"Introducing Madama Da Luna,"
said Ms. Vortex.
"Ooh!" whispered Tera.
"She's perfect!"

For once, Pelly agreed with Tera.

Madama Da Luna *was* perfect.

She smiled a perfect smile.

She waved a perfect wave.

Then she took off her scarf . . .

Pelly couldn't believe it!
Madama Da Luna had
a fluffy, fabulous fluffernobbin.
It swayed with the music as she sang:
"Laaaaa-HA-HA-HA-baaaaa!"
When she was done, everyone cheered.
"I'm going to be an opera singer, too,"
said Tera. "LAA-BAA-HAA!"
Madama Da Luna smiled.
"Keep practicing, dear."

“How do you do it?” asked Horus.

“It’s my fluffernobbin,” said Madama Da Luna.

“It helps my range and gives
my voice that something special.”

“Mine, too?” Pelly asked.

“Try it, darling.”

“Laaaaa-HA-HA-HA-baaaaa,” Pelly sang.

“Beautiful!” said Madama Da Luna.

And from then on,
Pelly didn't mind
being a little different.
After all, special martians
usually are.